The Pug Who Wanted to Be a Reindeer

Also by Bella Swift

The Pug Who Wanted to Be a Unicorn

The Pug

Who Wanted to Be a

Reindeer

BY Bella Swift

ALADDIN New York London Toronto Sydney New Delhi

With special thanks to Anne Marie Ryan
Illustrations by Nina Jones and Artful Doodlers

This book is a work of fiction. Any references to historical events, real people, or real places are used fictitiously. Other names, characters, places, and events are products of the author's imagination, and any resemblance to actual events or places or persons, living or dead, is entirely coincidental.

ALADDIN

An imprint of Simon & Schuster Children's Publishing Division
1230 Avenue of the Americas, New York, New York 10020
First Aladdin hardcover edition September 2021
Text copyright © 2019 by Orchard Books
Illustration copyright © 2019 by Orchard Books
Originally published in Great Britain in 2019 by The Watts Publishing Group
Also available in an Aladdin paperback edition.
For information about special discounts for bulk purchases, please contact Simon & Schuster Special Sales at 1-866-506-1949 or business@simonandschuster.com.
The Simon & Schuster Speakers Bureau can bring authors to your live event.
For more information or to book an event contact the Simon & Schuster Speakers Bureau at 1-866-248-3049 or visit our website at www.simonspeakers.com.
The text of this book was set in Bembo Std.
Manufactured in the United States of America 0821 FFG
2 4 6 8 10 9 7 5 3 1
Library of Congress Control Number 2020949485
ISBN 9781534486829 (hc)
ISBN 9781534486812 (pbk)
ISBN 9781534486836 (eBook)

Contents

Chapter One

Peggy the pug's flat, black nose twitched as she napped on the sofa. As carols played softly on the radio and the spicy scent of gingerbread wafted from the kitchen, Peggy dreamed about Christmas. It was her favorite time of year—because it was in December last year that she'd found her home.

The sound of the front door opening jolted Peggy awake.

"We're home!" cried a voice from the hallway, followed by the thud of backpacks dropping to the floor.

Chloe! thought Peggy, scrambling to her feet. Curly little tail wagging, she raced out to the hallway as fast as her short legs could carry her.

"Hi, Peggy!" cried Chloe, a dark-haired girl wrapped up in a coat and a woolly scarf. She crouched down on the floor to stroke Peggy's tan-colored fur.

"I miss you *sooooooo* much when you're at school!" Peggy told her best friend. Of course to Chloe it just sounded like barking, but Peggy covered Chloe's face with kisses so she understood.

"Let me pat Peggy too," said Chloe's little sister, Ruby. She was clutching a paper snowman decorated with cotton balls. Kneeling down next to Chloe, she patted Peggy on the head.

SLURP! Peggy licked Ruby's hand affectionately, catching a faint taste of glue. Chloe was Peggy's best friend, but Peggy loved the rest of the family too, and missed them all when they weren't at home.

This autumn, there had been lots of changes in the Jackson family. Ruby had started going to the kindergarten at Chloe's school, Finn was at high school now, and Mum had opened her very own café. Dad worked from home sometimes, like today, but mostly Peggy was at home on her own.

"How was school, girls?" said Dad, coming out of the kitchen with a smudge of flour on his nose.

"Okay," said Chloe, shrugging her coat off and hanging it on a peg.

Hmm, thought Peggy, cocking her head to the side and studying her friend. *That's strange.* Normally Chloe chattered about the fun things she'd learned at school, and the games she'd played at break time with her friends.

"Bad," said Ruby. "Miss Roberts is horrible and scary. She's a meanie."

"Of course she isn't," laughed Dad.

"She has a loud, scary voice and she likes to tell children off," insisted Ruby.

Chloe unzipped her little sister's coat and helped her hang it up. "I thought Miss Roberts was a bit scary when I started kindergarten. But actually, she's very kind and a really good teacher."

"That's right," said Dad, nodding. "It took Chloe a while to settle in at kindergarten, too. But once she made friends with Ellie, she was very happy there."

The smile faded from Chloe's face, like a cloud covering up the sun.

What's wrong? wondered Peggy.

"Let's go and hang your snowman up," said Dad.

Peggy and the girls followed him into the kitchen, where he pinned Ruby's snow-man up next to an advent calendar. Trays of gingerbread cookies shaped like stars, reindeer, and Christmas trees were cooling on the kitchen counter.

"Mmm," said Chloe. "Those smell good, Dad. Can we have some for our snack?"

"Yes, but only one each," said Dad. "They're for the bake sale at the school Christmas fair tomorrow."

Peggy's big brown eyes stared up at Chloe pleadingly as Chloe munched her gingerbread. *Please, please, please*, Peggy's eyes begged. *Just a teeny-weeny bit?*

"You know I can't resist you, Peggy," said Chloe, snapping a piece off her cookie and giving it to Peggy.

Result! Peggy wolfed down the gingerbread.

"Want to watch *Sparkalina*?" Ruby asked her sister, heading into the living room and switching on the television. Peggy trotted after them and sat down happily in front of the TV. A beautiful cartoon unicorn flew across the screen, singing the show's theme tune.

But Chloe shook her head. "Not in the mood," she said, trudging upstairs.

Now Peggy was sure there was something

wrong. *Sparkalina* was Chloe's favorite television program. If she didn't want to watch it, something *must* be worrying her.

Peggy climbed up the stairs. Chloe's bedroom door was shut, but Peggy could hear muffled sounds coming from inside.

Nudging the door open with her paw, Peggy saw Chloe curled up on her bed, sobbing into her pillow. Peggy clambered up onto the bed and nestled against Chloe.

"Today was such a bad day," sobbed Chloe, burying her face in Peggy's fur. "Ellie doesn't want to be my friend anymore. There's a new girl named Hannah in my class, and now the two of them are doing everything together. They sat together at lunchtime and picked each other for partners in PE."

Peggy licked the salty tears off Chloe's cheeks. She hated to see her friend so upset.

"I feel so left out," wailed Chloe, hugging Peggy tight. "Christmas is going to be so awful if I can't do fun things with Ellie."

You've got me, thought Peggy. *I'll always be here for you.*

Last Christmas, Chloe's family had taken Peggy home from a dog shelter. It was meant to be just for a week, but because of her special friendship with Chloe, the Jackson house had become Peggy's forever home. Peggy owed everything to Chloe—and she would do anything to make Chloe happy.

Sniffing, Chloe wiped away her tears and sighed. "Thanks, Peggy," she said, planting a kiss on the pug's wrinkly head. "I feel a bit better now."

As Chloe started doing her math homework, Peggy heard a commotion coming from downstairs and went to investigate.

Finn, Chloe's teenaged brother, was in the kitchen with his friend Zach, eating gingerbread cookies. The boys were in a band together called Avocado Toast. At least, Peggy thought that was what it was called now. They had also been called Velvet Spaceship, the Hammerhead Sharks, and Gandalf's Beard. The band seemed to change its name on a weekly basis.

"We've had this gig booked for weeks," said Finn. "Playing at the school Christmas fair is a big deal for the band. You can't let us down."

"I'm sorry, man," said Zach, shrugging.

"I can't do it. I'm training for a charity race. Ten kilometers is a long way to run, and I've only got a week to get ready."

"If you don't play the gig, you're out of the band!" said Finn angrily.

"Fine!" shouted Zach. "Then I quit!" He grabbed his guitar case and stormed out of the house.

"What's all this shouting?" said Dad, coming into the kitchen holding his laptop. He stared at the crumbs on the now empty cooling racks. "And who's eaten all the gingerbread?"

"Sorry, Dad," said Finn. "I was hungry."

"Great!" said Dad, looking cross. "I don't

have time to make more because I've got to finish this presentation for work. Now what am I going to bring to the school fair?"

A short while later, Mum came home from the café, dropping a bag of food containers onto the kitchen table.

"Dinnertime!" she called up the stairs.

As they all sat around the table, Mum unpacked the plastic containers of sandwiches, sausage rolls, and salads.

"Leftovers from the café again," complained Finn.

"Business still slow?" Dad asked Mum.

Mum nodded, looking worried. "I barely had any customers today."

Chloe picked at her food listlessly, even though she usually loved sausage rolls.

She's still upset about Ellie, thought Peggy.

"I'm sure business will pick up," said Dad, "once word gets around and people taste your delicious food."

"I hope so," said Mum gloomily. "Otherwise I won't be able to repay the bank loan."

"Mummy," said Ruby. "For Christmas can I have a scooter? Oh, and a new teacher?"

"Christmas!" Mum groaned, burying her head in her hands. "As if we didn't have enough to worry about already. I can't believe it's only two weeks away."

Peggy looked from one member of her family to another. Christmas was supposed to be the happiest time of the year. So why did everyone look so sad and worried?

Chapter Two

"Can we go to the Christmas fair now, Daddy?" asked Chloe the next morning. "I've finished my homework."

"Not yet," said Dad, who was vacuuming the living room.

"But I want to see the reindeer," whined Ruby.

Chloe and Ruby had been excited about their school fair for weeks. As well as lots of fun Christmas crafts and stalls where they could buy presents, there were going to be real, live reindeer!

When Dad had finished his chores, he and the girls put on their coats.

"Take me too," whimpered Peggy. Mum was at the café, and Finn had already gone to the fair to set up his drum kit. Peggy didn't want to be stuck at home on her own.

"Can we take Peggy, Dad?" asked Chloe.

"That's not a bad idea," said Dad. "She could use a walk."

Hooray! thought Peggy as Chloe clipped on her lead.

"We need to stop at Mum's café on the way and pick up some treats for the cake stall," said Dad.

Walking briskly because it was cold, they headed into the town center and stopped outside a small café with a sign that said TASTY TREATS.

Dad pushed the door open and they all stepped into the warmth. Looking around, Peggy saw a glass cabinet filled with a mouthwatering display of cakes, pastries, and sandwich fillings. There was a bright red poinsettia on every table, and

garlands of gold tinsel decorated the walls.

This is lovely, thought Peggy.

But Mum, who was wiping down the counter, didn't look very cheerful.

"Oh dear," said Dad. "Is it still slow?"

Mum nodded gloomily. "I've only had two customers this morning."

"Everyone's probably doing Christmas

shopping," said Chloe. "They'll come in later on."

"I hope so," said Mum. She reached underneath the counter, pulled out a box, and handed it to Dad. "Here are some mince pies for the school fete." Sighing, she added, "It's not as if I'll need them at this rate."

They left the café, and Peggy trotted by Chloe's side as they walked to the primary school.

"Oh, wow!" said Chloe as they entered the school auditorium. It had been transformed into a winter wonderland, with snowflake decorations hanging down from the ceiling. Children shrieked excitedly, spending their pocket money on sweets, face-painting, and the secondhand-toy stall, while their parents sipped mulled wine and chatted. The school choir was singing carols on the stage as Finn and his bandmate, Jasmine, set up their instruments.

"Can we go outside and see the reindeer?" asked Chloe.

"Sure," said Dad. "I'm going to drop the mince pies off at the cake stall."

Holding Peggy's lead, Chloe guided Ruby through the crowded auditorium and out to the playground.

A pen had been set up on the playing field, and inside it two big animals were nibbling the grass.

"Reindeer!" cried Ruby, running over to the pen.

Chloe joined the children clustered around the fence. Peggy stuck her head through the railings and peered up at the reindeer. Their thick, shaggy fur was light brown, and they had velvety antlers.

"Holly is the smaller one," explained the reindeer handler, "and Noel is the one with bigger antlers."

Peggy gaped at the reindeer. She thought they were beautiful.

"It's rude to stare," said Noel.

"Sorry," said Peggy. "I just love your ant–ers."

"Why, thank you," said Noel. "They *are* looking rather impressive this year."

"I like your curly tail," said Holly.

The reindeer handler gave Chloe and Ruby some slices of carrot, and the girls offered them to the reindeer on their palms.

"Carrots again," sighed Noel. "I really fancied mushrooms or some brussels sprouts."

"That tickles," giggled Chloe as Holly's soft lips nuzzled her hand to gobble up the carrot.

"Reindeer come from near the North Pole," the reindeer handler informed the children.

"Don't they get cold?" asked Ruby.

"Their fur keeps them warm," said the reindeer handler. "And they have specially shaped hooves to help them walk on snow."

Peggy peered at the reindeer curiously. "Where are your wings?" she asked them. She wondered if the wings were tucked up against the reindeer's sides.

"Er, what wings?" asked Holly, confused.

"I thought reindeer could fly?" said Peggy. Chloe had told Peggy stories about Rudolph and the other reindeer flying Santa's sleigh through the sky on Christmas Eve.

Noel snorted with laughter, but Peggy didn't understand what was so funny.

"We don't need wings," said Holly, kindly, "because we're magic." She winked at Noel.

"Oooooh," said Peggy, feeling a bit silly. "Have you ever met Santa Claus?"

"No," said Noel. "But we did meet Comet and Cupid once."

"Comet was really nice," said Holly, munching a carrot slice. "But Cupid was a bit of a show-off."

"Oh, you're just jealous because she complimented my antlers," said Noel.

Peggy had lots more questions she wanted to ask the reindeer, but Chloe tugged gently on her lead. "We've got to go back inside," Chloe told Ruby. "Finn's band is playing now."

Back in the auditorium, a crowd had formed around the stage. Chloe picked Peggy up so she could see better.

"We're Avocado Toast," Finn shouted into the microphone. "Are you ready to rock?"

The crowd whooped in reply. Peggy barked and wagged her tail. Finn clicked his drumsticks together three times to count Jasmine in. "And a one . . . and a two . . . and a—"

Finn pounded his drums as Jasmine played the keyboards and sang. But without Zach on guitar, they sounded terrible.

Ouch! thought Peggy. Her ears hurt from the horrible racket.

"BOO!" called the audience.

"Oh no," muttered Chloe.

At first Peggy thought she was talking about Finn's band, but then Peggy followed Chloe's gaze. She was staring at two girls in matching Christmas sweaters. Peggy recognized Chloe's friend Ellie. But who was the other girl?

"Ellie's with Hannah again," Chloe whispered into Peggy's ear. "I've got to get out of here. I can't face seeing them together." She handed Peggy's lead to Ruby and slipped away, looking upset. Peggy longed to go after her friend, but she knew Chloe wanted her to stay and look after Ruby.

As the boos from the audience got louder, Finn's band stopped playing.

Poor Finn, thought Peggy, watching him pack up his drum kit, his cheeks flaming with embarrassment.

Suddenly, Ruby tugged on Peggy's lead. "Come on, Peggy. We've got to go— NOW!"

Peggy's paws nearly got trodden on several times as Ruby hurried through the crowd to the soft-toy stall—a table piled high with secondhand cuddly toys.

"Any animal you want for a dollar, sweetie," the lady running the stall told Ruby.

Instead, Ruby dived under the table.

"We've got to hide in here," Ruby whispered to Peggy, "because I saw Miss Roberts." She peeped out nervously, checking to see if her teacher had gone, then ducked back in. "She's still out there."

Peggy snuggled up next to Ruby. *I might as well make myself comfortable*, she thought. Who knew how long they'd be hiding out?

A little boy came over to the soft-toy table. He looked around at all the toys, trying to make up his mind.

"How about this purple hippo?" said the stallholder. "Or a fluffy duck?"

"No," said the boy. "I want a doggie."

Good choice! thought Peggy, letting out a yip of approval.

The boy crouched down and peered under the table. His eyes landed on Peggy and widened.

"I want this one!" he said, picking Peggy up.

Hey, thought Peggy, her legs flailing, *I'm not a toy!*

"That's MY dog," said Ruby, trying to snatch Peggy away from the boy.

"I saw her first!" cried the boy, refusing to let go.

Soon Ruby, the little boy, and Peggy were all howling.

"Peggy!" cried Chloe, running over. Peggy wriggled out of the boy's arms and ran to her friend, barking with relief. She'd never been so happy to see anyone!

Chloe quickly explained the situation to the little boy's mum. The lady running the stall found a toy pug for him. He was still sniffling, but when his mum said, "Let's go and get a mince pie from the cake stall, Archie—I hear they're delicious." he soon cheered up.

"Can we go home now, Chloe?" Ruby asked.

Chloe sighed. "Good idea."

They found Dad and helped Finn pack up his drum kit. Then they all trudged home miserably. *Oh dear*, Peggy thought. Even the Christmas fair hadn't managed to cheer her family up!

Chapter Three

That night, Peggy tossed and turned on Chloe's bed, but it wasn't because of the strong winds blowing outside. She couldn't fall asleep because she was worried. Chloe had been so unhappy after the school fair, and even cuddles from Peggy hadn't cheered her up. . . .

What can I do to help? wondered Peggy.

As she lay awake next to Chloe, thinking about the fair, Peggy remembered what Holly and Noel had told her about reindeer being magic. If Peggy were magic too, she could make Chloe and her family happy for Christmas. *That's it!* Peggy thought, sitting up in bed, her whiskers quivering with excitement. *I'll become a reindeer!*

Snuggling up against Chloe again, Peggy wondered if she'd still be able to sleep on her friend's bed when she was a reindeer. *I'll probably be too big*, she realized. That made her feel a bit sad, but it was a sacrifice Peggy was willing to make to become magic. It was the best way she could think of to help the person she loved most in the world. Relieved that she had a plan, Peggy finally fell fast asleep.

The next morning, Peggy stared at her reflection in the mirror on the back of Chloe's closet door. Her tan fur was almost the same color as the reindeer's, but that was where the similarities ended. Peggy frowned, making her forehead even more wrinkled. *I need antlers*, she thought.

She headed downstairs for breakfast.

Chloe, Ruby, and Finn were already in the kitchen, eating pancakes.

"Do you want to invite Ellie over to play this afternoon?" Mum asked Chloe.

"No!" Chloe shook her head. When Mum looked at her curiously, Chloe added, "She's, um, busy."

"Then you can all help me with the chores," announced Dad.

The children groaned, but Dad said, "There was a storm last night, so I need you kids to rake up the debris."

After breakfast, Peggy followed the children out into the garden. The lawn was strewn with leaves and twigs that had

blown down in the gales overnight. A big, striped ginger cat was sitting on top of the garden fence.

"Hi, Tiger," Peggy called up to him.

Tiger just narrowed his green eyes and sniffed in a superior manner.

When she'd first come to live with Chloe, Peggy had hoped she'd make friends with the neighbor's cat. But Tiger wasn't very friendly. The only reason he came into her garden was to poo behind the bushes.

Finn and Chloe started raking up the

leaves, while Ruby gathered twigs and sticks and put them in a pile.

Ooh! thought Peggy. *Those look like antlers. . . .*

She dragged a twig off the pile.

"No, Peggy," said Ruby. "I can't play fetch with you right now." She pulled the twig out of Peggy's mouth and put it back on the pile.

When Ruby's back was turned, Peggy tried again, dragging another twig off the pile. *How can I get this on?* she wondered, prodding the stick with her head.

"What are you doing, Pig Tail?" sneered Tiger, looking down on her.

Peggy ignored the cat. She was determined to attach her antlers somehow.

"Naughty Peggy!" said Ruby crossly. She tried to yank the stick away, but Peggy bit down, unwilling to let go of it.

"Drop!" ordered Ruby.

No, thought Peggy.

Finally, with one strong tug, Ruby yanked the stick out of Peggy's mouth.

Peggy flew back and fell—*PLOP!*—into the huge pile of leaves Finn and Chloe had raked up. Leaves flew up into the air and scattered around the garden.

As she shook off the leaves, Peggy ignored the sound of Tiger's mocking laughter.

"Oh great," grumbled Finn. "Now we have to rake everything up again."

"I'll put Peggy inside," said Chloe. "So she doesn't get in the way."

Chloe carried Peggy into the kitchen and shut the door behind her.

SLAM!

Oh dear. Now Chloe was cross with her, and Peggy was still no closer to becoming a reindeer.

The next day, Peggy was home alone. Mum and Dad were at work and the children were at school. Peggy felt bored and lonely.

She'd spent the whole morning trying to think of a way to become a reindeer but hadn't had any ideas.

When she wandered into the kitchen for a drink of water, her eyes fell on the vegetable rack. *Aha!* she thought, spotting a bunch of carrots. Noel and Holly had eaten carrots at the Christmas fair. *Maybe if I eat enough carrots, I'll turn into a reindeer.* It was definitely worth a try.

She worked the carrots out of the rack with her paws.

CRUNCH! CRUNCH! CRUNCH! They weren't her favorite food—or even her second-favorite—but Peggy munched carrot after carrot until every single one was gone.

I'll take a nap, thought Peggy. *Hopefully, when I wake up, I'll be a reindeer.*

GROOOOAAAAAN.

"We're home!" called Chloe.

Peggy staggered to her feet. Her belly churned and her head felt dizzy. *I must be transforming into a reindeer,* she told herself.

She stumbled into the hallway to greet Chloe and—

BLUUURGH! Peggy threw up all over the floor.

"Ew," said Ruby, holding her nose.

"Looks like Peggy got into the carrots," sighed Dad, looking down at the orange puddle.

"Oh, you poor little thing," cried Chloe, picking Peggy up.

Wait a minute, thought Peggy. Reindeer were big. If Chloe could still pick her up, it meant her plan hadn't worked. Despite eating a whole bunch of carrots, she was still a pug. Peggy whim-pered, feeling terrible.

"Don't worry, Peg," said Chloe, stroking her head. "I'll take care of you."

As Dad cleaned up the mess, Chloe gave Peggy some

water and took her upstairs. She held Peggy on her lap, stroking her back.

"I had a bad day too," Chloe whispered. "I heard Ellie and Hannah talking about how much fun they had at the school fair." She sighed sadly. "I was really looking forward to doing fun stuff with Ellie over the Christmas holidays, but she only wants to hang out with Hannah."

Now it wasn't just Peggy's tummy that hurt. Her heart ached too.

I have to find a way to become a reindeer, she thought. *I need magic to make Chloe happy again.*

Peggy's tummy felt much better the next day, but she still hadn't found a way to become a reindeer. After school, Chloe and Ruby were making Christmas cards in the kitchen. Peggy sat by the table, watching them paint.

"Is that card for Ellie?" asked Ruby, dipping her paintbrush into yellow paint.

Chloe shook her head. "We're not friends anymore," she told her sister sadly. "It's for my teacher."

Ruby wrinkled her nose as she painted a gold star. "I'm not making a card for

Miss Roberts. She's a horrible meanie."

Chloe laughed. "She's not horrible. She's just a bit strict."

Ruby peered at Chloe's painting of Santa and his sleigh. "Why does that reindeer have a red nose?"

"Duh," said Chloe. "It's Rudolph. He's Santa's most magical reindeer."

Peggy's ears perked up with interest. *Hmm,* she thought. *Maybe if I had a red nose, I'd be as magical as Rudolph!*

Peggy watched Chloe dab red paint onto a jolly-looking Santa. Suddenly, she knew what to do! She leaped up onto the table and knocked the yellow and green paint

onto the floor as she buried her nose in the pot of red paint.

"Hey!" cried Chloe. "What are you doing?"

Peggy looked up, dripping red paint all over the girls' cards. *Am I a reindeer now?* she wondered hopefully. She glanced at her reflection in the oven door. A pug with paint all over her furry face stared back at her.

"My cards!" wailed Ruby. "Peggy ruined my Christmas cards."

Dad ran into the kitchen. "What a mess!" he groaned, looking at the paint-splattered floor. Sighing, he went to fetch the mop.

"Come on, Peggy," said Chloe, scooping her up. "Let's go and get you clean."

Looking over Chloe's shoulder as they headed toward the bathroom, Peggy stared down at the cards she'd spoiled. She'd made a mess of everything . . . again.

There were less than two weeks until Christmas, and Peggy still hadn't made her family happy. It was time to face the facts. She needed a new plan . . . fast!

Chapter Four

Peggy woke up bright and early the next morning. The school run was always one of her favorite parts of the day. She loved trotting alongside Dad and the girls, sniffing the sidewalk and chatting to other dogs. But today she was even more excited than usual because she had come up with a brilliant new plan—if Peggy couldn't become a reindeer herself, she'd just have to find Santa and ask him to help!

But first, she needed to talk to Holly and Noel. They'd met Comet and Cupid, so they might know how Peggy could find Santa. Hoping that the reindeer would still be at Chloe's school, so she could sneak in and ask them, Peggy bounded downstairs. She was too excited to eat breakfast. But nobody else was in a very good mood. . . .

"What the heck!" said Finn, sounding cross. "There's paint on my school shoes."

Oops, thought Peggy.

Finn checked his phone, then shoved it angrily back into his jacket pocket. "Nobody's replied to my ad for a new guitarist yet."

The mail plopped through the slot. Mum picked up the envelopes and groaned. "Look at all these bills."

"Where's Ruby?" asked Dad. He called up the stairs, "Ruby! It's time for breakfast!"

A few minutes later, there was still no sign of Ruby.

"Ruby!" bellowed Dad. "Come down or you'll be late for kindergarten!"

"I've got to go," said Mum. "I can't be late opening up the café."

"I'll walk with you," said Finn, slinging his schoolbag over his shoulder. "Since I'm not talking to Zach."

Peggy helped Chloe and Dad search for Ruby. They looked under the dining room table, in the laundry hamper, and behind the living room curtains. There was no sign of her downstairs, so they went upstairs, calling her name.

"She'd better not make me late for school," grumbled Chloe, checking behind the shower curtain. "My class is going to the pantomime today." Then she muttered,

"But it probably won't be any fun because Ellie and Hannah have already said they're sitting together."

Normally Peggy loved playing hide-and-seek, but today she was impatient to get to school. So she followed her nose.

"She's here!" barked Peggy, discovering Ruby hiding under her parents' bed.

"Out you come," Dad ordered Ruby.

"I don't want to go to school!" wailed Ruby as Dad picked her up and carried her downstairs. "I don't like Miss Roberts."

As Dad ushered Chloe and Ruby out of the house, Peggy tried to follow them. "Sorry, Peg. We're running late, so I'm driving the girls to school today." He put Peggy in the garden and shut the gate.

"No!" yelped Peggy. She gazed around the garden in dismay. *I need to talk to the reindeer! I have to get out of here!*

Peggy tried to open the gate with her paws. She pushed and pushed with all her might, but the gate didn't budge.

She heard someone sniggering behind her. Peggy whirled around and saw Tiger strutting along the fence.

"Going somewhere, Pig Tail?"

Peggy ignored the cat and batted the

gate with her paws again, feeling desperate.

Tiger looked amused. "That's never going to work," he said. "Why don't you just jump?" The cat crouched on his haunches and leaped down, landing nimbly on the ground.

"Tiger, you're a genius!" exclaimed Peggy.

"Yes, I know," said the cat, cleaning his whiskers with his paw.

Peggy backed up and started running toward the fence. *Here goes!* she thought, leaping into the air.

BOINK! She crashed right into the fence.

"Ouch!" Peggy groaned, her head throbbing.

"That's got to hurt," Tiger said, his green eyes glittering mischievously. "Maybe you should try climbing over. Watch. . . ." He scrambled up over the garden fence, his sharp claws clinging to the wood. "Your turn!" he called down.

Peggy tried to copy what the cat had done. Jumping up, she pawed at the fence, but her claws weren't sharp enough to grip the wood.

OOF! She fell back on her bottom. "This is useless," she sighed. "I'm stuck here."

"Why do you want to escape, anyway?"

asked Tiger. "I thought you liked all those annoying children."

"I love them," Peggy corrected the cat. "That's why I need to get out of the garden—to help them."

Tiger sniffed. "My motto is 'Every cat for himself.'"

"Well, I'm not a cat," said Peggy, staring down at the ground sadly. *Of course!* she thought. The answer was right under her nose.

Dogs might not be good at climbing and jumping the way cats were, but they were great at digging. She could tunnel her way out of the garden!

Peggy ran over to the fence at the back of the garden, squeezed between two bushes, and began to dig. Her paws churned up soil as she tunneled through the damp, cold earth.

"Ooh," said Tiger, tutting. "Mr. Jackson is going to be so cross. You know how proud he is of the garden. He hates it when I do my business in the shrubs."

Peggy ignored him and kept digging. Soon there was a mound of earth piled up by the fence. *Is the hole big enough yet?* wondered Peggy, panting with exhaustion. She tried to get through but she didn't quite fit. *Keep digging*, she told herself.

Peggy dug and dug. Taking a deep breath, she tried again. She stuck her head into the hole and pushed her furry little body through the tunnel.

SNAP! Peggy felt her collar break as she burrowed into the narrow tunnel, but

she didn't stop. She wriggled through the soil like a worm until—*POP!*—her head emerged on the other side of the fence.

Peggy staggered to her feet and shook herself all over to get the dirt off. She'd done it!

Looking around nervously, Peggy realized something—she'd never been beyond the garden on her own before.

Tiger peered down at her from the top of the fence. "Well . . . what are you waiting for?"

Peggy thought about her house and felt sad. She remembered what it had felt like to be alone in the world, before her family adopted her. Peggy didn't want to leave the home that she loved so much, but she knew she had to find Santa. He would make Chloe happy again, and the rest of the family too.

Resisting the urge to go straight back to

her garden, Peggy told herself to be brave. She trotted down the alley and out onto the street. Her nose to the sidewalk, she sniffed the ground, following a familiar scent. She walked and walked until—*BUMP!*—her nose hit a wall.

I must be at school now, Peggy thought.

Jumping up, she pressed her nose against the glass to look through the window. To her surprise, she didn't see Chloe or Ruby—or any other children. But she did see Mum, holding a tray with two cups of tea on it. She was bringing it to a table where two ladies wearing gym clothes sat eating bacon sandwiches.

This wasn't school—it was Mum's café!

Peggy's mouth watered as she stared at the sandwiches, but she knew she couldn't stop for a snack. She quickly jumped down from the window before Mum spotted her. There was no time to waste. She was on a mission—she needed to get to school and speak to the reindeer!

Chapter Five

Peggy looked from right to left, trying to remember the way they'd walked from the café to school on the day of the Christmas fair.

It's this way, she decided, setting off down the street.

She passed a newsstand, a hair salon, and a pharmacist, but soon the shops gave way to houses. As she walked along, Peggy admired the pretty wreaths decorating the doors. One house even had a huge inflatable snowman on the lawn!

When she came to a crossing, Peggy wasn't sure which way to go. She thought for a moment. *I'd better turn right*, she reasoned. *Because I want to go the right way.*

Feeling very clever, she turned right every time she came to a crossing. Soon all the houses began to look the same to her.

Oh, wow, thought Peggy. *There's another house with a snowman.* She stopped and took a closer look. The inflatable snow-man had a black top hat and a carrot nose, just like the one she'd seen before. There was a tricycle in the front garden, and a red car parked in the drive, just as there had been at the other house. *Wait a minute*. . . .

This was the very same snowman she'd

seen before! *I've been going around in circles!* she suddenly realized.

Peggy sniffed the ground. She could smell all sorts of interesting scents, but she couldn't catch even the faintest whiff of her family.

Peggy's paws ached and her tummy rumbled. She regretted not eating any breakfast. Exhausted, she plopped down on the edge of a front garden for a rest. *Face it*, she told herself. *You're lost.*

WOOF! WOOF! WOOF!

An enormous Doberman came thundering across the grass, his ears pricked up and his eyes flashing.

"GET OFF MY LAWN!" he growled, straining on the long rope that was attached to his spiked collar.

Terrified, Peggy leaped to her paws. For a second she stood frozen, too scared to move.

The massive dog bared his sharp teeth, slobber dripping from jaws big enough to swallow Peggy in one bite. "What are you

waiting for?" he snarled, lunging forward menacingly.

Without looking, Peggy ran straight into the street.

HONK! HONK! HONK!

A car swerved out of the way, narrowly missing Peggy.

"Stupid mutt!" the driver shouted out the window angrily.

Peggy raced to the other side of the road and collapsed on the sidewalk. Then she began to sob.

"Do you have a death wish or something?" asked a voice coming from above her.

Sniffling, Peggy looked up. A squirrel sat

on a tree branch overhead, studying her
with beady black eyes.

"Oh dear," he said sympathetically, scam-
pering down the tree trunk. "It can't be
as bad as you think it is. Now, dry those
eyes," he went on, using his fluffy gray tail
to wipe away Peggy's tears, "and tell Andy
what's wrong."

"I'm lost," wailed Peggy. "I was trying to
find Chloe's school, but I went the wrong
way."

"What's a school?" asked the squirrel.

"It's where lots of children go to learn and play," explained Peggy.

"Oh," said Andy. "I know where that is—in fact, I was just heading there myself. Want to come with me?"

"Yes, please," yelped Peggy, relief flooding through her. "That would be amazing." She scrambled to her feet and hurried after the squirrel, whose tail bobbed ahead of her.

"Hey!" she panted, as something occurred to her. "I thought squirrels were supposed to be scared of dogs."

"I saw you run away from that big dog," Andy said, and chuckled, his whiskers twitching. "You're about as scary as a butterfly."

The squirrel scampered through a set of big iron gates. He headed across the grass to a cluster of trees and scratched his head with his paw. "I know I buried some acorns around here a few months ago. Now, where was it . . . ?"

Peggy gazed around her, confused. "Um . . ."

"Oh, sorry," said Andy. "I nearly forgot. The school's over there," he said, pointing with one of his paws, before bounding off in search of his nuts.

Peggy hurried off in the direction Andy

had pointed. Soon, she heard the excited shrieks of children playing. But when she got there, her heart sank. There were lots of children swinging on swings, spinning on a merry-go-round, and dangling from monkey bars. But this wasn't a school—it was a playground. Andy had taken her to the park!

"Doggie!" cried a little girl, spotting Peggy from the top of the slide. She whooshed down and then ran out of the playground to give Peggy a cuddle.

Soon, a cluster of toddlers had gathered around Peggy.

"She's so cute," said a little boy, feeding Peggy one of his rice cakes.

"Her face is all wrinkly," said a little girl, "just like my grannie's." She gave Peggy an apple slice.

Peggy wagged her tail and enjoyed the attention as the little kids stroked her fur and shared their snacks with her. Soon, her belly was full.

"I hope Santa Claus brings me a puppy," said a little boy, patting Peggy on the head.

Santa! thought Peggy in alarm, suddenly remembering what she was supposed to be doing. She needed to find Holly and Noel! After bolting down a final piece of cheese sandwich, she wriggled away from the little kids and ran to the park gates.

She decided to head away from where she and Andy had come from. As she walked, she noticed a girl carrying a backpack— just like the one Chloe took to school.

I'll follow her, thought Peggy. *She's probably going to school.*

She trotted after the girl. Before long, the girl turned down a front path and rang the doorbell of a house with a red door. A lady opened the door and gave the girl a hug. "Hi, honey," she said. "How was school?"

Uh-oh, thought Peggy. School was over for the day. The gates would be locked. Now she wouldn't be able to ask Holly and Noel for help. This was a disaster!

As Peggy trudged along the quiet streets, trying to work out what to do next, Christmas trees glowed from the front rooms of the houses she passed. Peggy swallowed hard, trying not to cry as she thought of her own cozy home. Chloe would be getting back from school and finding Peggy gone. Peggy knew her friend would be terribly worried about her. *I only left so I could help Chloe*, thought Peggy.

She glanced up at the sky. It was already beginning to get dark. In the gloomy twilight, Peggy saw something in the distance that made her heart leap—a magnificent

reindeer standing on the roof of a house. It must have flown up there!

She ran to the house. "Excuse me!" she called up to the reindeer.

The reindeer stayed silent and aloof, not even glancing down at her.

Peggy tried again. "Hello! I'm hoping

that you might be able to help me find Santa Claus. . . ."

Suddenly, the reindeer lit up and its red nose started to flash.

It was just a decoration.

Oh no, thought Peggy, watching the glowing reindeer in dismay. *How will I ever find Santa now?*

Chapter Six

Peggy sat down on the cold sidewalk. All she wanted to do was go home, but she had no idea how to get there. Besides, she still had to find Santa.

"You're not a quitter," Peggy told herself sternly. She thought for a moment. The reindeer handler had said that reindeer came from near the North Pole—so that must be where Santa lived too.

But which way was north? As she was trying to decide which way to go, Peggy heard a loud crash. It seemed to have come from behind the house.

Peggy jumped up in alarm and peeked nervously down the side passage. In the moonlight, she could see two trash cans. One had been knocked over, and its contents were strewn all over the ground. Over the rubbish loomed the shadow of a huge . . . terrifying . . . WOLF!

Peggy gasped.

The wolf's pointy ears twitched. As it turned its head to look at her, Peggy saw that it had reddish fur, a black nose, and a bushy tail. It was much smaller than its shadow because it wasn't a wolf at all—it was a fox!

"How do you do?" said the fox. "I'm Vicky." She dabbed her whiskers daintily with the back of her paw and gestured to a pile of rotting eggshells, fish bones, and moldy banana peel. "Would you care to join me for supper? There's more than enough to go around."

"Er, no thank you," said Peggy. Mum and Dad were always complaining about foxes, but Peggy was surprised. For a wild animal, Vicky seemed very polite. Peggy went over and sat down next to her, trying to ignore the reek of rotten food.

"What are you doing out here at night?" asked Vicky. "You don't look like a stray. Don't you have a home?"

"Yes," said Peggy sadly. "But I can't go back until I've found a way to help my family."

"I understand," said Vicky, nodding. "I have three dear little babies of my own. I'd do anything for them." She gestured to a chicken carcass with her paw. "Chicken is my favorite, but I'm saving this for the kiddies back in my den. Are you trying to find dinner for your family?"

"No, I'm trying to find Santa Claus," said Peggy. "He lives near the North Pole. Have you ever been there?"

Vicky shook her head. "But I do have a distant cousin who lives in the Arctic region. I believe that's near the North Pole."

"Do you know how to get there?" Peggy asked eagerly.

"Hmm," said Vicky, thinking. She glanced up, and Peggy followed her gaze. It was a clear night, and stars shone brightly in the dark sky.

"We foxes use the stars to guide us on

our way," explained Vicky. "Do you see that very bright star—just underneath the moon?" She pointed with her paw.

Peggy nodded.

"That's the North Star. If you follow it, I'm sure you'll find your way to the North Pole."

Peggy gazed in wonder at the North Star, twinkling like a diamond against the inky black sky. "Thank you very much," she told the fox. "You've been so helpful. I suppose I'd better be heading off now."

"Are you sure you don't want a bite to eat before you go?" asked Vicky, offering Peggy a pile of potato peelings. "You've got a long journey ahead of you."

"Er, no, thank you," said Peggy. "Save it for your babies."

With the North Star lighting her way, Peggy set off for the North Pole. It was bitterly cold and her paws were sore, but Peggy didn't mind. Each step she took was taking her closer to Santa!

As she walked, Peggy kept her eyes on the sky. Soon enough, Santa Claus would be flying across it on his Christmas Eve journey, delivering presents to all the good boys and girls. Peggy hoped she'd be able to reach the North Pole before then, as she hated the thought of Chloe being unhappy on Christmas Day. Peggy remembered how delighted Chloe, Finn, and Ruby had been last year, when they'd opened their presents.

The evening wore on and the sky grew cloudy, dimming the starlight. Something cold and white landed on Peggy's nose. A snowflake!

I must be getting closer to the North Pole, thought Peggy as snow began to fall, dust-

ing the sidewalk with fluffy white flakes. Soon, it got harder and harder for Peggy's short legs to trudge through the snow. By now, the sky was too overcast for Peggy to see the North Star.

I can't go any farther, Peggy realized. She climbed onto the doorstep of the nearest house. Shivering, she curled up in a ball and whimpered softly, longing to be snuggled up with Chloe in her warm bed.

The door opened. An elderly lady in a fluffy purple dressing gown and slippers stood in the doorway. "I thought I heard something," she said, peering down at Peggy through her glasses. "Oh, you poor little thing. You'd better come inside."

Gratefully Peggy staggered into the warmth and light. The lady bent down slowly, picked Peggy up, and carried her

into the living room. After setting her down on the plump sofa, in front of a flickering gas fire, the lady wrapped Peggy in a knitted blanket.

"I'll fix you something to eat while you warm up," said the lady, disappearing into the kitchen.

Soon, Peggy heard sausages sizzling. Her tummy began to rumble as she realized she hadn't had anything to eat since the playground.

When the lady returned, she set a plate of sliced sausages on the floor in front of the fire. Wriggling out from under the blanket, Peggy jumped down and gobbled the sausages up in a few bites, then licked the plate clean.

"My Charlie used to love sausages too," said the lady. She sighed deeply. "He was a beagle. I'd love to get another dog, but my arthritis is too bad for me to manage all the walks."

Peggy nuzzled the lady's hand, wanting to say thank you.

"I'm Sue," said the lady, "but what's your name?" She felt around Peggy's neck. "Hmm. No collar. You're a Mystery Pup."

Now that she'd warmed up and her belly was full, Peggy looked around Sue's living room. By the window, a little artificial

Christmas tree sat on a table, its colored lights flashing. Above the fire, the mantelpiece was filled with framed photographs, most showing three children with red hair and freckles.

Her knees creaking, Sue lowered herself onto the sofa and picked up a basket of yarn. She patted the seat next to her. "Come up here," she told Peggy. "I get so lonely on my own. It's nice to have some company for a change."

Peggy joined Sue on the sofa. As she knitted, Sue chatted to Peggy about her grandchildren. "My son lives far away," she explained, "so I don't get to see the little ones as often as I'd like."

Peggy felt sorry for Sue. She loved being part of a big family. With a pang of sadness, she thought about Chloe, Finn, and Ruby, and hoped they weren't too worried about her.

"I'm going to visit them soon," continued Sue. "I always make them each a Christmas sweater. They've just had a new baby"— Sue pointed her knitting needle toward a photo of a chubby baby with a shock of red hair—"and I'm making her one too."

Looking down at Peggy, Sue tapped her chin thoughtfully. "Actually . . ." She pulled the sweater over Peggy's head and pushed her front paws through the armholes. "It's the perfect size for you!"

Sue rummaged around in her basket and pulled out more wool. "You can have that one," she said. "There's still a week until Christmas. I've got plenty of time to make another sweater for the baby."

Peggy could tell that Sue loved her family as much as Peggy loved hers. It was hard to be apart from the people you loved the most. *Will I ever be able to help them?* she wondered.

Cozy in her new sweater and exhausted from her long day, Peggy felt her eyelids begin to grow heavy. Soon, the comforting clickety-clack of Sue's knitting needles lulled her into a deep sleep.

In her dreams, an old man dressed in a red suit with a black belt and big, black boots appeared. He had a snowy-white beard and wore a red hat with a white pom-pom.

"Ho ho ho!" chuckled Santa, holding his round belly. "Don't ever give up hope, Peggy." He peered at her through his glasses, his blue eyes twinkling merrily. "Remember, Christmas is the most magical time of year. . . ."

Chapter Seven

Peggy woke to the smell of something delicious. Yawning, she stretched her legs and wondered why they felt so sore. And what on earth was she wearing? Had Ruby dressed her up in dolls' clothes again? Suddenly, everything came flooding back to her. She wasn't at home—she was at Sue's house.

Peggy jumped down from the sofa and wandered into the kitchen.

"Good morning, Mystery Pup!" said Sue cheerfully. She was dressed in a velvety tracksuit and was frying bacon on the stove.

Peggy looked up at her with mournful, pleading eyes. Chloe could never resist this look—but would it work on Sue?

A moment later, Sue placed a plate heaped with bacon on the floor, next to a bowl of water.

Yes! Peggy could hardly believe it was all for her.

"No bacon for me, I'm afraid," said Sue, pouring herself a bowl of bran flakes. "My doctor says I need to lower my cholesterol."

When Peggy and Sue had finished breakfast, Sue picked up the telephone. "I'd better make an appointment with the vet. It's early, but the office should be open. The vet will be able to check your microchip and find your owner."

No! thought Peggy. As tempting as it was to go home, Peggy knew she couldn't let Sue take her to the vet. Santa Claus had told her not to give up—and she wouldn't.

I've got to get out of here, Peggy thought. She went over to the door and pranced around in circles, whining, hoping that Sue would get the hint.

"Oh, silly me," said Sue. "You need to do a piddle." Unlocking the door, she let Peggy into the garden.

It was a cold, clear winter's morning. A blanket of snow sparkled in the sunshine, making the garden look like a beautifully iced cake.

As soon as she'd finished doing her business, Peggy sprinted across the lawn, the snow crunching under her paws.

"Come back!" cried Sue.

But Peggy didn't stop, or even look back. She ran down the sidewalk until she'd left

Sue's house far behind. She felt bad, as Sue had been very kind to her, but she needed to find Santa Claus—he was the only one who could help her family.

Suddenly, Peggy skidded to a stop. Running along the neatly shoveled sidewalk was the very man she was looking for!

He looked exactly like he had in her

dreams—with a red suit and hat and a curly white beard. The only difference was that he was wearing sneakers instead of black boots.

"Santa!" barked Peggy. "I need to talk to you!"

But Santa must not have heard, because he ran right past her.

"Santa, wait!" barked Peggy, hurrying after him.

For a tubby man, Santa could run surprisingly quickly. Peggy's little legs struggled to keep up with his long strides. She watched his back, which had the number twenty-one pinned to it, disappear as he ran through some gates. Panting,

Peggy hurried after him. Running through the gates, she looked around. But there was no sign of Santa anywhere.

"Oh no!" wailed Peggy in despair. She sat down on the chilly path. She'd come so close, only to fail.

"Oh, hello again," said Andy the squirrel, hopping over to Peggy across the snow. "Are you still looking for the school?"

Peggy suddenly realized she was in the same park she'd been in yesterday. It looked so different covered in snow that she hadn't recognized it at first.

"No," said Peggy, shaking her head. "Now I'm searching for Santa Claus."

"What does he look like?" asked Andy.

"He's got a red suit and a white beard," said Peggy. She sighed. "I nearly found him, but he was running too fast and I lost him."

"Well, you're in luck," said Andy. He pointed with his paw. "Because he's right over there."

Peggy turned around and saw Santa Claus run through the gates.

Then another Santa came sprinting into the park.

And another one!

Peggy stared in disbelief as Santa after Santa jogged past. As they puffed and panted, their breath sent clouds of steam into the cold air. Some were tall, and some were short. Some had big bellies, while others were lean. A few were wearing headphones, and others

clutched water bottles. And unless Peggy was mistaken, some of them were ladies. But they were all wearing red hats and suits with numbers pinned to their backs.

"Stop!" Peggy barked, chasing after the pack of Santas. "Which one of you is the real Santa Claus?"

None of the runners even slowed down. In fact, some people in the park were urging them to go even faster.

"Come on!" cheered a lady wearing reindeer antlers. "You can do it!"

"Please help me!" yapped Peggy. "It's really important!"

"Get lost!" shouted one of the Santas

angrily. "I'm almost at the finish line."

Peggy knew that one couldn't be the real Santa—he was much too grumpy. But Santa *had* to be somewhere in this pack of red-suited runners. If they wouldn't stop, she'd just have to make them.

Taking a deep breath, Peggy pushed past the cheering people. She darted through the sea of red legs and stopped in the middle of the path. "SANTA!" she barked as loud as she could.

"Whoa!" cried a Santa wearing neon-green sneakers. He swerved to avoid Peggy, but crashed into another Santa.

BUMP! That Santa crashed into

another Santa, and soon there was a
pileup on the path. Red hats and white
beards flew into the air as the runners
tumbled on top of each other and landed
in a heap. Some of the Santas picked
themselves up and carried on running.

A Santa with friendly brown eyes looked down at Peggy.

"Hey, I know you," he said. He took off his white beard, and Peggy recognized Finn's friend Zach, who used to be the guitarist in the band. Zach frowned. "What are you doing out here by yourself?"

A girl wearing snow boots ran up to them. "That's Peggy!" she cried. Peggy recognized her, too—she was Chloe's friend Ellie.

"Peggy went missing the other day," Ellie explained to Zach. She gestured with a gloved hand to a nearby tree. Pinned to the trunk was a handmade poster with a picture of Peggy on it. "When I saw the posters, I knew I had to help look," said Ellie, scooping Peggy up. "Chloe must be so upset."

Chloe! thought Peggy with a pang. To her surprise, Ellie looked just as worried about Chloe as Peggy felt. *That's funny*, thought Peggy. *I thought she didn't want to be Chloe's friend anymore. . . .*

Zach nodded. "Yeah, Finn will be really worried, too. He loves the Pegster."

"I couldn't help overhearing," said the lady wearing reindeer antlers who had been cheering on the runners. "Why don't I give her owners a call?" She took a cell

phone out of her coat pocket and dialed the number on the poster.

Uh-oh, thought Peggy. She tried to wriggle out of Ellie's arms, but Ellie held her firmly. "No you don't," she told Peggy. "You're not going anywhere except home. I bet everyone's worried sick about you."

Peggy felt awful. She'd wanted to make her family happy, but all she'd done was make them even more upset. She hadn't reached the North Pole. She hadn't even managed to make it out of her own town! Her mission had been a hopeless failure.

"Help, Santa!" barked Peggy desperately, as the last of the red-suited runners crossed the finish line. "I need a Christmas miracle! Please use your magic to make Chloe and her family happy again!"

Chapter Eight

"There she is!"

Peggy's ears pricked up at the sound of a familiar voice. Peering over Ellie's shoulder, she saw Chloe sprinting toward her, with Finn right behind. Mum and Dad, holding Ruby's hands, were hurrying down the path after them. And they all had huge smiles on their faces!

Peggy wriggled so much that Ellie had to put her down. Ears flapping and tail wagging, Peggy ran toward her family.

"Oh, Peggy!" cried Chloe, scooping her

up and hugging her tight. "We were all so worried about you."

"Nice outfit, Pegster," said Finn, patting Peggy on the head.

"My turn!" said Ruby, jumping up and down. Chloe bent down so her little sister could stroke Peggy too.

Peggy's heart felt like it was going to burst. Her family wasn't angry with her for running away. They just seemed overjoyed to have her back.

"Thanks so much for finding Peggy," said Mum to the lady with the cell phone.

"It's these two you should thank," said the lady, gesturing to Ellie and Zach.

Mum suddenly did a double take. "Miss Roberts! I didn't recognize you with your reindeer antlers on."

Ruby looked up from patting Peggy and froze when she recognized her teacher.

Miss Roberts smiled. "My friend was running in the race, so I thought I'd cheer her on." She crouched down. "Is it okay if I stroke Peggy, too?"

Ruby nodded nervously.

Miss Roberts tickled Peggy behind the ears, and Peggy licked her hand.

"You're so lucky to have Peggy," said Miss Roberts. "I'd love to get a dog, but I live in an apartment without a garden."

"You like animals?" asked Ruby shyly.

Her teacher nodded. "I love animals. I have a cat named Willow."

As Ruby told her teacher all about Peggy, runners wearing medals and proud smiles began to make their way out of the park.

"I'm sorry you didn't get to finish the race," Finn said to Zach.

"That's okay," Zach said, shrugging. "I did most of it. Besides, some things are more important than getting a medal." He coughed awkwardly. "How's the band?"

Finn shrugged. "We still don't have a guitarist. . . . You interested?"

Zach grinned. "Sure. Playing in a band is a lot more fun than running."

The boys exchanged a high five.

"I'm thinking we should change our name," said Finn. "What do you think about 'Maximum Velocity'?"

That's terrible, thought Peggy.

"I love it!" said Zach.

"I guess we can take these down now," said Dad, going over to the tree and removing the poster with Peggy's picture on it.

"They worked, though," said Ellie.

Chloe smiled at her shyly. "Thanks for helping to find Peggy."

"Of course I helped," said Ellie. "You're

my best friend, after all. And always will be."

Awww, thought Peggy as they hugged.

While Chloe and Ellie chatted happily, Peggy spotted another little dog over by the playground—a tiny terrier, with shaggy brown hair and a red bow on her head. She strained on her lead, which was held by a girl around Chloe's age.

The terrier wagged her tail eagerly, as if she wanted to play.

Peggy wandered over to say hello, giving the other dog a friendly sniff.

"Hi, I'm Princess," said the terrier. "Don't judge—I didn't choose the name."

"It's nice," said Peggy.

And so was Princess. Soon, the two dogs were rolling around in the snow, barking and playing.

"Peggy!" cried Chloe, running over. "For a second I thought I'd lost you again."

She looked at Princess's owner in surprise. "Hannah? What are you doing here?"

"Ellie told me about your dog going missing, and I wanted to help look for her," said Hannah. "I know how upset I'd be if I lost Princess."

Chloe crouched down and gave Princess a pat. "She's really cute."

"Thanks," said Hannah, smiling. "It looks like she and Peggy are friends already. Do you think we could be friends too?"

"I'd like that," said Chloe, smiling back at her.

Linking arms, Chloe, Ellie, and Hannah went back to the rest of Chloe's family, with Princess and Peggy following behind them.

"Everyone's invited back to Tasty Treats on High Street," called Mum. "There's a free mince pie for everyone who did the Santa run!"

An hour later, Mum's café was so busy that every single seat was taken and the windows were fogged up with steam. Ellie, Chloe, and Hannah shared a table, drinking hot chocolates with mounds of whipped cream, as Princess gnawed on a dog treat. Runners in Santa suits scoffed sandwiches,

hungry after their long run. Ruby, who was wearing her teacher's reindeer antlers, sat with Miss Roberts and her friend, munching mince pies.

Dad and Finn helped Mum serve customers. Peggy jumped down from Chloe's lap and trotted by Dad's heels as he placed a cup of tea in front of an elderly lady.

"Why, it's you!" said Sue, staring at Peggy in astonishment. "Mystery Pup."

"Do you know Peggy?" asked Dad.

"She spent last night at my house," explained Sue. "I found her shivering on my porch. I took her in and gave her that sweater to wear."

"Well, that's one mystery solved," said Dad, chuckling. "We were wondering where she got her sweater." He beckoned Mum over and introduced Sue.

"Thank you so much for taking care of Peggy," said Mum. "She could have frozen to death out in the cold."

"Oh, it was no trouble at all," said Sue. "I live on my own, so it was nice to have some companionship."

Dad nodded. "I think Peggy ran away because she was lonely. My wife recently opened this café, the kids are all at school now, and I've been really busy with work."

"No, that's not it," barked Peggy. "I was trying to find Santa!"

But of course the humans didn't understand her.

"Well, I know what it's like to be lonely," said Sue. "I miss having a dog, so it was lovely to spend time with Mystery Pup." She smiled. "I mean, Peggy."

"Yes," said Mum. "Dogs always cheer a place up." Suddenly, a thoughtful expression crossed her face. "You know, that gives me an idea. . . . People love being around dogs. And most cafés don't allow them. Maybe I should turn this place into a dog-friendly café."

"That's a brilliant idea!" said Dad. "You

could take Peggy to work with you so she doesn't get lonely at home."

Peggy wagged her tail. She liked it here in the café, surrounded by friendly people, and her new friend, Princess.

"I'll definitely come here for a cup of tea if I can get some cuddles with Peggy," said Sue.

Peggy rubbed against Sue's leg, happy to oblige.

"I go running with my Labrador every morning," said one of the Santas, over-hearing. "I'd love to come here with him afterward."

"You should change the café's name

to 'Bones and Scones,'" suggested Zach, through a mouthful of mince pie.

"No, I've got a better idea," said Finn. "You can call it 'Pups and Cups.'"

"I love it!" said Mum.

And Peggy did too!

Back at home that night, they all decorated the Christmas tree together.

"We've all been so busy," said Mum, hanging a shiny Santa-shaped bauble on a branch, "that we forgot the true meaning of Christmas."

"Presents?" asked Ruby.

"No, silly," said Dad, tousling her hair. "Family."

"Too bad it took losing Peggy to make us realize that," said Finn.

Chloe picked Peggy up and hugged her. "Don't ever leave us again, Peggy. We missed you so much when you were gone."

"But we got her back!" said Ruby, putting her reindeer antlers on Peggy and giving her a kiss.

Mum took a picture of the children and Peggy. "Lovely! That can be our family Christmas card."

"Aww," said Chloe, smiling. "Peggy looks so cute as a reindeer."

But Peggy knew she didn't need to become a reindeer anymore. Her family loved her just as she was. Looking around at their beaming faces, Peggy let out a howl of joy.

Thank you, Santa, she thought, watching the Santa-shaped ornament twinkle merrily in the fairy lights. His Christmas magic had worked. The people Peggy loved most in the whole world were happy again, and she was safely back home with them.

It wasn't the twenty-fifth of December yet, but Peggy had everything she wanted for Christmas already.

Can't get enough of Peggy?
Here's a sneak peek at
her next story....

Sunlight streamed through the kitchen windows as Peggy the pug's family ate their breakfast. As usual, the little dog sat by Chloe's chair, her big brown eyes gazing up at the curly-haired girl imploringly. Peggy loved every member of her family, but

Chloe was Peggy's special friend. She was also the most likely to share her breakfast!

Peggy whimpered quietly and wagged her curly tail. Chloe slipped Peggy a piece of bacon under the table, and Peggy gobbled it down. *Yum!*

"You know you're not supposed to feed Peggy from the table," Dad scolded Chloe over the top of his tablet.

"Why not?" protested Peggy. Crispy bacon was soooo much tastier than dog food! But to her family, Peggy's words just sounded like barking. Humans couldn't understand animal language.

"But you and Mum are always saying

how important it is to share," said Chloe, giving her dad a cheeky grin. "Anyway, I can't help it. Peggy looks so cute."

Chloe's little sister, Ruby, looked down at Peggy and cooed. "Who's the cutest doggie in the whole world? Is it Peggy? Yes, it is!"

Finn, Chloe's older brother, snapped a close-up of Peggy's face with his phone. "I'm tagging it #pugmug," he said, sharing it on his social media.

Peggy sighed happily. She loved weekends, when all three children were at home.

Dad put down his tablet and smiled. "Good news! The forecast says it's going to be sunny all weekend. I've got a lot to do in the garden. The spring greens are starting to come up, but I want to sow some carrots and runner beans."

"I love springtime," said Chloe. "It's my birthday, and then the Easter Bunny comes!"

"Actually," said Mum, sipping her coffee, "Easter comes first this year."

"But my birthday was before Easter last year," said Chloe.

"Easter isn't on the same day every year, dummy," said Finn.

"This year your birthday is the week after Easter," explained Dad.

"That reminds me," said Mum. "I want to make some hot cross buns for the café, but I was thinking of trying out some exciting flavors." Mum had recently opened a dog-friendly café called Pups and Cups. "Any ideas?"

"Smoky bacon flavored!" barked Peggy, though of course Mum didn't understand her. The café was good for dogs, so Peggy thought the snacks should be too!

"Unicorn hot cross buns," suggested Ruby.

"Interesting . . . ," said Mum.

"You should make spicy ones," said Finn, shaking some hot sauce onto his scrambled eggs. Lately, Finn added extra-hot spicy sauce to everything. Chloe had told Peggy that he did it because he thought it made him look tough.

"Gross," said Chloe, wrinkling her nose. "Nobody wants to eat a bun that will make their eyes water. Make triple-chocolate ones—with white, milk, and dark choco-late. Mmm. . . ."

"Those are all great ideas," said Mum. "I'll test them out today."

"I'll help!" Ruby offered eagerly.

"Can I ride my bike to Ellie's house?" asked Chloe. "She invited me and Hannah over yesterday at school. She said she had something exciting to show us."

"That's fine," said Mum. "What do you suppose it is?"

"Ooh! Maybe she's got a unicorn!" said Ruby.

"Yeah, I'm sure it's that," said Finn, rolling his eyes.

"Hannah and I tried to get her to give us a hint," said Chloe, "but she just twitched her nose mysteriously."

"Maybe she was hinting that you smell bad," laughed Finn.

"You're the one who stinks!" said Chloe,

giving her brother a shove. "Your feet smell like a cross between moldy cheese and rotting fish."

"Okay, okay, that's enough," said Dad. "I could use some help in the garden today. Any volunteers?"

Finn shrugged. "I'll help."

Chloe laughed. "That's going to make you even stinkier!"